## Ladybird Readers

CW00350795

# The Empty Pot
# Activity Book

Written by Hazel Geatches
Illustrated by Gustavo Mazali
Song lyrics on page 16 by Wardour Studios

 Singing *    Reading    Speaking    Critical thinking

 Spelling    Writing    Listening *

*To complete these activities, listen to tracks 2, 3, and 4 of the Reader audio download available at **www.ladybirdeducation.co.uk**

**1** Match the words to the pictures.

1 leaves

2 plant

3 pot

4 seed

5 palace

6 the emperor

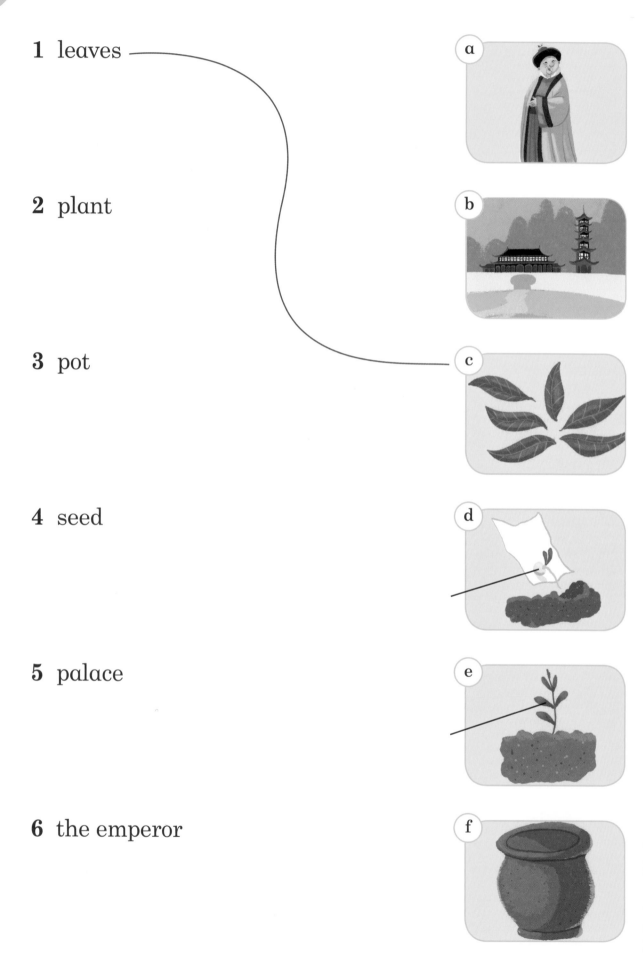

a

b

c

d

e

f

## 2 Look and read. Circle the correct words.

1    The emperor is (old.) / young.

2    Jun is **old.** / **young.**

3    The soil is **bad.** / **good.**

4    The seeds are **good.** / **bad.**

5    Jun is the **new** / **old** emperor.

6    Jun's mother and father are **sad.** / **happy.**

## 3 Who says this?

the emperor

Jun

Jun's father

Jun's mother

1 "I'm old. I have no child."                    the emperor

2 "You grow beautiful plants,
  Jun. Go to the palace."

3 "That's good soil and water."

4 "Don't worry."

5 "I like this empty pot."

**4** Talk about the picture with a friend.
Use *There is* and *There are.* 🗨

**1** There is a big palace.

**2** . . . a beautiful garden.

**3** . . . lots of boys.

**4** . . . one empty pot.

# 5 Circle the correct pictures.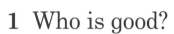

1 Who is good?

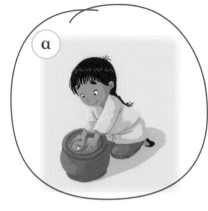 

2 Who is old?

3 Who is happy?

4 Who gets the seeds?

5 Who is the new emperor?

## 6 Listen, color, and draw.
## Use the colors below. 🎧*

**Look and read. Circle the correct words.**

**1**

**a** sad

**b** see

**c** seed

**2**

**a** plant

**b** palace

**c** pot

**3**

**a** seed

**b** soil

**c** leaves

**4**

**a** pot

**b** put

**c** boy

8

**8** **Draw a picture of Jun. Read the questions and write about Jun.**

1 What is your name?

My name is Jun.

2 Where do you live?

I live in

3 Who do you live with?

I live with

4 What do you do at home?

At home, I

## 9 Find the words. Write the words.

paanthas(pot)thasyfloweredfatheriobboystheysenmothershasemperorest

1 ........... pot ...........

2 ....................

3 ....................

4 ....................

5 ....................

6 ....................

## 10 Ask and answer questions about the pictures with a friend. Use the words in the box. 🗨

| garden | leaves | seed | pot |
|---|---|---|---|

**1**

Where is the emperor?

He is in the garden.

**2**

What does the emperor give Jun?

He gives him a . . .

**3**

Where does Jun put the seed?

He puts it in a . . .

**4**

What do the boys see in their pots?

They see . . .

## 11 Look, match, and write the words.

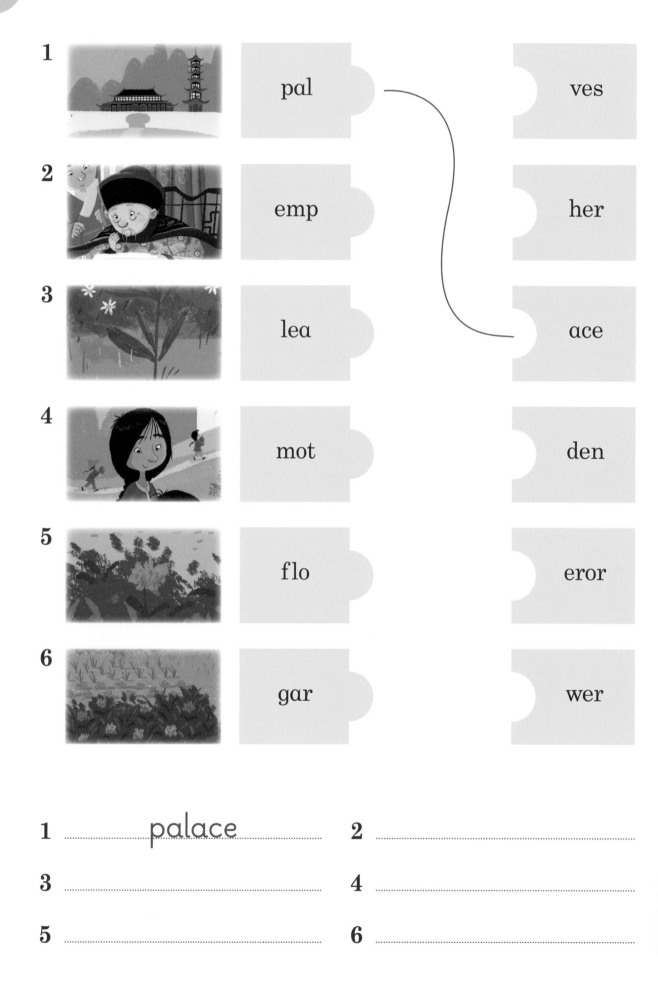

1    pal             ves

2    emp             her

3    lea             ace

4    mot             den

5    flo             eror

6    gar             wer

1   palace        2 _____

3 _____        4 _____

5 _____        6 _____

**12** **Listen, and put a** ✓ **by the correct sentences.**

**1 a** "I have a child." ☐

   **b** "I have no child." ✓

**2 a** "Come to my garden and get a seed, please." ☐

   **b** "Come to my palace and get a seed, please." ☐

**3 a** "Go home. Put it in a plant." ☐

   **b** "Go home. Put it in a pot." ☐

**4 a** "I like this empty pot." ☐

   **b** "I don't like this empty pot." ☐

**5 a** "My seeds are old and bad." ☐

   **b** "My seeds are new and bad." ☐

**6 a** "Well done, Jun! You're a bad boy!" ☐

   **b** "Well done, Jun! You're a good boy!" ☐

**13** Look and read.
Write the correct words on the lines.

| sitting | carrying | watching | walking |

**1**

The emperor is
_____sitting_____ in
his garden.

**2**

Jun is _____
to the palace.

**3**

Jun is _____
his pot.

**4**

The boys are
_____ their
pots to the palace.

14

## 14 Look at the letters. Write the words.

**1**

p r m o r e e

The _____emperor_____ is in his garden.

**2**

p e l c a a

"Come to my _____ and get a seed, please."

**3**

e v l a s e

The boys see _____ in their pots.

**4**

r a f h t e

"Don't worry," says his _____.

**5**

t m y e p

"I like this _____ pot."

## 15   Sing the song. *

"I am old," said the emperor.
"I need a new emperor here.
I can give the boys some seeds.
I need an emperor in a year."

The empty pot, the empty pot . . .
Can Jun's plant grow a lot?
The empty pot, the empty pot . . .
"Come and show me what you have got!"

"Put these seeds in a pot," said the emperor.
"Can you make them grow?
Come back in a year and show them to me.
My seeds are bad, but you do not know!"

The empty pot, the empty pot . . .
Can Jun's plant grow a lot?
The empty pot, the empty pot . . .
"Come and show me what you have got!"

  *To complete this activity, listen to track 4 of the Reader audio download available at **www.ladybirdeducation.co.uk**